KATIE WOO

Rules the School

by Fran Manushkin

illustrated by Tammie Lyon

capstone

Katie Woo is published by Picture Window Books
A Capstone Imprint
1710 Roe Crest Drive
North Mankato, MN 56003
www.capstonepub.com

Library of Congress Cataloging-in-Publication Data
Manushkin, Fran.
  Katie Woo rules the school / by Fran Manushkin; illustrated by Tammie Lyon.
       p. cm. — (Katie Woo)
  Summary: Combines four previously published stories, including Katie and the class pet, No more teasing, The big lie, and Star of the show, in which Katie Woo deals with problems at school.
  ISBN 978-1-4048-7908-9
  1. Woo, Katie (Fictitious character)—Juvenile fiction. 2. Schools—Juvenile fiction. 3. Chinese Americans—Juvenile fiction. [1. Schools—Fiction. 2. Chinese Americans—Fiction.] I. Lyon, Tammie, ill. II. Title. III. Series: Manushkin, Fran. Katie Woo.
  PZ7.M3195Kbj 2012
  [E]—dc23   2012003135

Photo Credits
Fran Manushkin, pg. 96; Tammie Lyon, pg. 96

Designer: Emily Harris
0412/CA21200580
Printed in China
032012 006679

Table of Contents

Katie and the Class Pet

One day, Miss Winkle asked, "Who would like to have a class pet?"

"I would!" yelled everyone.

"I want a pony," said Katie. "We could ride him at recess!"

"A pony is too big," said Miss Winkle. "We need a pet that fits in our room."

"How about a rabbit?" asked JoJo.

"Or a mouse," said Pedro.

"I'll think about it," said Miss Winkle.

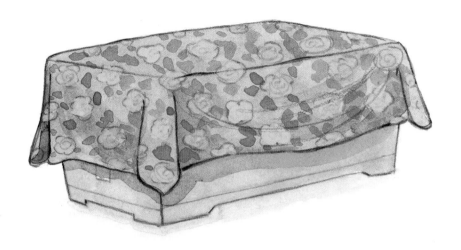

A few days later, Miss Winkle
came in with a cage.

"Our class pet is inside," she said.
"Can you guess what it is?"

"A bunch of ants?" asked Pedro.

"A skunk?" joked Barry.

"Surprise!" said Miss Winkle.
"It's a guinea pig."

"He's so cute," said JoJo.

"Let's name him Binky," said
Katie. "The name is cute and little,
like him."

"Binky! Binky! Binky!" everyone shouted.

"Binky it is!" said Miss Winkle.

Binky let everyone hold him.

He made happy, squeaky noises.

He liked being at school. He
loved music time best. He always
squeaked along.

Every Friday, Miss Winkle took
Binky home for the weekend. But
one Friday, she said, "I'm going away
this weekend. I need someone to take
Binky home."

"Me! Me! Me!"
yelled everyone.

Miss Winkle pulled a name from a hat. Katie Woo won!

"Binky, I'll take good care of you," she promised.

Katie put Binky's cage in her room.
She fed him guinea-pig pellets and
grapes and cucumbers.

Then she and Binky played games.

"Keep the doors and windows closed," said Katie's dad. "We don't want Binky to get lost."

That night, Katie fell asleep in her
bed, and Binky slept in his house.

Katie played with Binky all weekend.

On Sunday, she said, "Binky, I'd love to keep you, but you belong to our class. They would miss you."

On Monday morning, Katie took
Binky out of his cage one last time.

"Uh-oh," she said. "I have to go to
the bathroom."

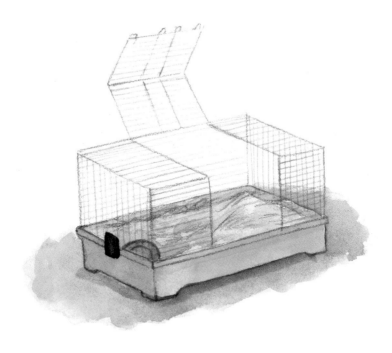

When Katie came back, Binky was
gone! Katie looked under the bed and
everywhere. No Binky!

The window was open a crack. "He
must have escaped!" Katie cried.

Katie felt terrible. "What will
I tell my class?" she said. "I promised
to take good care of Binky."

Katie picked up her backpack and
headed out the door.

Katie walked to her classroom slowly. "I hope I never get there," she said.

But she did.

Miss Winkle asked, "Katie, how was your weekend with Binky?"

"Um, I have some bad news . . ." Katie began.

Then she started to cry.

Suddenly, Katie felt something on her neck. It was warm and soft. It was Binky, poking out of her backpack!

"So that's where you went!" Katie smiled. "You were getting ready to come to school!"

"Katie," asked Miss Winkle, "what's the bad news you were going to tell us?"

"It's not bad anymore!" Katie laughed. "It's funny!"

And she told them the whole happy story.

No More
Teasing

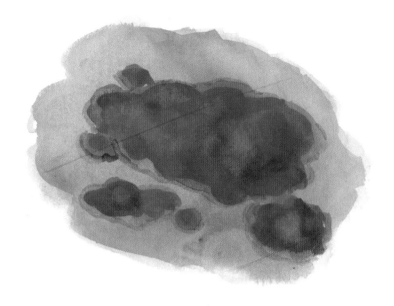

One day, on the way to school,
Katie Woo tripped. She fell into the
mud. *Splat!*

She scraped her knee, and mud
got on her new sweater and all of her
books.

Katie started to cry.

"Cry baby! Cry baby!" yelled Roddy Rogers.

Katie's feelings were so hurt, she cried harder.

Roddy grinned.

At school, Roddy Rogers kept
teasing Katie during recess.

"Go away!" she told him.

But Roddy didn't.

At lunch, they had pizza, Katie's favorite.

She took such a big bite that she got tomato sauce on her nose and cheek.

"Look at Katie," Roddy shouted.
"Katie's got a goopy face!"

Roddy said, "Goopy face! Goopy
face!"

"Stop it!" cried Katie. But Roddy
didn't stop. He was having too much
fun.

Roddy made faces
at Katie all day long.

When Katie stuck
her tongue out at
him, he made
more faces. Ugly ones.

"How can I make Roddy stop teasing me?" Katie asked her friend JoJo.

But JoJo didn't know.

The next day, Roddy teased Katie when she was running at recess. And he teased her when she was trying to read her book.

Katie was so unhappy. She didn't
want to go to school anymore.

The next day, Miss Winkle told the class, "Everyone, our butterflies are ready to hatch. Please hurry over and watch them!"

Katie pushed up her glasses.

"Hey, I see four eyes!" Roddy said
in a quiet voice. He knew if Miss
Winkle heard him, he would get in
trouble.

Katie was about to say something back. But suddenly, her butterfly began hatching.

It was so amazing. She couldn't take her eyes off it!

Roddy said, "Four eyes!" a little louder.

But Katie kept watching her butterfly.

Roddy was so mad. He slammed his desk and hurt his finger.

Later, the class worked on their "Good Neighbors" paintings with a partner.

Roddy snuck over to Katie and said, "Ew! Your painting is ugly!"

But Katie loved painting so much that she kept doing it.

"Hey!" Roddy said. "Didn't you hear me?"

Katie still didn't answer.

Roddy got so mad that he smeared black paint all over his part of his picture.

"Hey!" his partner yelled. "You ruined our painting!"

On the way home, Roddy glared at Katie, but she didn't even look at him.

Katie began smiling and smiling. When JoJo sat down, Katie told her, "I'm so happy! I know how to make Roddy stop teasing me."

"What do you do?" asked JoJo.

"Nothing!" Katie said. "When I don't cry or yell, Roddy isn't having fun, so he stops teasing me."

"Katie Woo, you are one smart girl," said JoJo.

"Thanks!" said Katie. And she smiled all the way home.

The Big Lie

One day after recess, Miss Winkle told the class, "Jake has lost his toy airplane. Has anybody found it?"

Katie Woo shook her head no. So did her friends Pedro and JoJo and everyone else.

"My father gave me the airplane yesterday," said Jake.

"It was a birthday present,"
he said.

"Maybe your plane flew away,"
said someone else.

"That is not funny," said Miss
Winkle.

JoJo told Jake, "I saw you playing with your plane at recess. It's so neat! I hope you find it."

Miss Winkle asked again, "Does anyone know where Jake's airplane is?"

"I don't," Katie told Jake. But she was lying.

Earlier that day during recess,
Katie saw Jake running around with
his airplane.

"I want to do that!" Katie told
herself. "I wish that plane belonged
to me."

When recess was almost over, three
fire trucks sped by.

While everyone was
watching them and
waving to the firefighters,
Katie grabbed Jake's plane.
She put it into her pocket.

Now Jake's plane was inside Katie's desk.

"I can't wait to play with it when I go home," Katie thought.

During art class, Katie said,
"Maybe a kangaroo hopped over and
put the airplane in her pouch."

"I don't think so," said Miss
Winkle. "There are no kangaroos
around here."

During spelling, Katie said,
"Maybe the garbage man came and
took Jake's plane."

"No way!" JoJo said. She shook her
head. "I didn't see any garbage trucks."

Jake kept staring at the empty
box that his airplane came in. The
birthday ribbon was still on the box.

Jake looked like he was going to
cry.

Katie didn't feel happy either.

When nobody was looking, she

took something out of her desk and

put it into her pocket.

Katie walked to the window and began using the pencil sharpener.

All of a sudden, Katie yelled, "I see Jake's plane. It's by the window! It must have flown in during recess."

Katie handed Jake the plane. She whispered, "That was a lie, Jake. I took your plane, and I am very sorry!"

At first, Jake was
angry at Katie. Then
he said, "I am glad
you gave it back. I feel
a lot better now."

"I do too!" Katie said.

And that was the truth.

Star of
the Show

Katie's class was putting on a play.

"We're doing *The Princess and the Frog,*" said Miss Winkle.

"Hooray!" said Katie. "I want to be the princess!"

"Me too!" yelled JoJo.

"I want to be the
frog," said Pedro. "I'm
a great hopper!"

"The parts are
on these cards," said
Miss Winkle. "Pick
one to see which part you get."

Katie picked
her card first.

"Oh, no!" she
groaned. "I'm not the
princess. I'm a worm!"

"I'm the princess!" yelled JoJo.

"And I'm the frog!" said Pedro.

"Good for you," said Katie. But she felt sad. "A worm cannot be a star," she sighed.

Katie told her dad, "It's no fun to be a worm. All I do is wiggle."

Her dad said, "You are crafty, Katie. You'll be a great worm."

Katie asked her mom, "What does crafty mean?"

"It means clever," said her mom. "I know you will be the best worm you can be!"

Katie tried to be a great worm.

She worked hard on her wiggling.

She wiggled forward, and she wiggled
backward.

Pedro and JoJo worked hard on their parts, too.

JoJo told Pedro, "Don't forget to kiss me so you can turn into a prince."

Pedro nodded. "Sure, sure."

The big day came, and the curtain went up.

"This is so exciting!" said Katie.

"Oh, Frog," called the princess.
"I threw my golden ball into the well.
Will you get it for me?"

"Sure!" croaked the frog. He began
hopping to the well.

"I can't see anything in my costume," said Katie.

She wiggled close to Pedro and almost tripped him!

"Oops," she thought. "That was not crafty."

"Thank you for bringing me my golden ball," said the princess.

"Uh-oh," Katie whispered. "The tree is swaying! It's going to fall down!"

Katie wiggled over and leaned on
the tree.

"Stop that!" hissed the tree. "I'm
swaying in the wind! I'm not falling
down!"

It was time for
the frog to kiss the
princess, but the
frog didn't move.
He looked scared.

"Kiss her!"
whispered Miss Winkle.

The frog still did not move. But Katie did!

She wiggled over and whispered, "If you don't kiss the princess, this worm will kiss YOU!"

"EW!" said Pedro.

He kissed the princess.

"You are now a prince!" she said.

The audience clapped and cheered,
"Hurray!"

As the princess took a bow, her crown fell off — and landed on the worm's head!

Katie smiled and
wiggled. Everyone clapped
harder! So Katie took a big
bow.

After the show, Pedro said, "Katie, you were so clever! You scared me into kissing JoJo."

"Well," said Katie, "I wanted you to be the best frog you could be."

"And you were the craftiest worm," said Katie's dad.

"I guess a worm CAN be a star!" said Katie.

And everybody agreed.

Having Fun with Katie Woo!

A Guinea Pig of Your Own

With this fun project you can make your own
guinea pig out of an old sock and some dryer lint!
Sounds crazy, right? But your pet will be *so* cute.
I promise!

What you need:

- an old, short sock

- stuffing, like cotton balls or fiberfill

- a needle

- thread

- craft glue

- dryer lint (Ask a grown-up where to find this soft, fuzzy
  stuff. It comes out of your clothes dryer!)

- googly eyes

- dark marker

What you do:

1. Fill your sock with stuffing. This will be your guinea pig's body, so make it as fat as you would like.

2. Tuck the top of the sock in, and then ask a grown-up to sew the hole shut with a needle and thread.

3. Working in small sections, apply some craft glue to the sock. Then cover the glue with dryer lint. Repeat until the whole sock is covered. Let dry.

4. To finish your project, glue googly eyes on your pet. With the marker, draw a nose on your pet.

You can even make your guinea pig a little bed lined with shredded paper, grass, or hay. Be sure to give your pet lots of love, but don't worry about feeding it!

Finger Puppet Fun!

Have you ever put on a puppet show? It is lots of fun and all of your friends will love it! Don't have any puppets? No problem! You can make your own. Choose from unique creatures or simple animals. It's up to you! Here's how . . .

What you need:

- Pipe cleaners in several colors
- Small pom-poms in several colors
- Small googly eyes
- Craft glue
- Wire cutters or scissors

What you do:

1. Firmly wrap a pipe cleaner around your finger to form the body. As you near your finger tip, make the coils smaller until the finger tip is covered. Carefully slip your finger out.

2. Glue a pom-pom onto the top of the body. You may need to hold it there while it dries.

3. Now glue two googly eyes onto the pom-pom.

4. Finally, add arms, ears, beaks, or other details using pieces of pipe cleaners. Cut the pipe cleaner with a wire cutter or scissors. Fold the pieces into the shape you want. Then glue or twist them onto your puppet. Try making a cat with short pointy ears, a rabbit with long ears, or a bird with wings and a beak.

Make two or three puppets, then act out a story with them. Your friends and family will love to watch your puppet show!

About the Author

Fran Manushkin is the author of many popular picture books, including *How Mama Brought the Spring*; *Baby, Come Out!*; *Latkes and Applesauce: A Hanukkah Story*; and *The Tushy Book*. There is a real Katie Woo — she's Fran's great-niece — but she never gets in half the trouble of the Katie Woo in the books. Fran writes on her beloved Mac computer in New York City, without the help of her two naughty cats, Miss Chippie and Goldy.

About the Illustrator

Tammie Lyon began her love for drawing at a young age while sitting at the kitchen table with her dad. She continued her love of art and eventually attended the Columbus College of Art and Design, where she earned a bachelors degree in fine art. After a brief career as a professional ballet dancer, she decided to devote herself full time to illustration. Today she lives with her husband, Lee, in Cincinnati, Ohio. Her dogs, Gus and Dudley, keep her company as she works in her studio.